BATMAN™

B… METROPOLIS

BY JOHN SAZAKLIS

ILLUSTRATED BY ANDY SMITH

COLORS BY BRAD VANCATA

BATMAN created by Bob Kane

SUPERMAN created by Jerry Siegel and Joe Shuster

HARPER FESTIVAL

An Imprint of HarperCollinsPublishers

HarperFestival is an imprint of HarperCollins Publishers.

Batman: Battle in Metropolis

HARP28042

Library of Congress catalog card number: 2012940915
ISBN 978-0-06-188537-2

Book design by John Sazaklis

13 14 15 16 17 SCP 10 9 8 7 6 5 4 3 2 1

❖

First Edition

THE HEROES AND VILLAINS IN THIS BOOK!

BATMAN

After being orphaned as a child, young Bruce Wayne vowed to fight crime and injustice throughout Gotham City, and so he became Batman! With his high-tech, crime-fighting gadgets and his armored vehicles, Batman fears no foe and is widely known as the World's Greatest Detective.

SUPERMAN

Sent to Earth from Krypton, Superman was raised as Clark Kent by small-town farmers and taught to value truth and justice. When not saving the world with his flight, super-strength, heat vision, and freezing breath, Clark is a reporter for Metropolis's newspaper the *Daily Planet.*

LEX LUTHOR

One of the smartest, wealthiest, and most dangerous businessmen in the world, Lex Luthor *was* the most powerful man in Metropolis . . . until Superman came along! Now Luthor uses his vast assets and scientific knowledge in an unending quest to eliminate the Man of Steel and take over the world.

THE JOKER

With an appearance caused by falling into a vat of toxic chemicals, the Joker is a brilliant prank engineer with a twisted sense of humor. His weapons are deadly party gags. One of them is his patented Joker Gas, a poisonous product that leaves victims with a garish grin across their faces. The Joker is Batman's greatest foe.

As night blankets all of Gotham City, Batman begins his vigilant crusade. He patrols the rooftops and alleyways in search of criminal activity. *Beep-beep!* An alarm on his mobile Batcomputer alerts him to a break-in at the Museum of Art and Science. Batman swings across the skyline using his Batrope to investigate the scene of the crime.

The Caped Crusader lands on the museum roof ready to confront the culprit. It is none other than the Joker! The Clown Prince of Crime has stolen a priceless green pendant from the meteorite exhibit.

"You're too late, Batman!" the Joker yells, climbing into his blimp. "Why don't you come back during regular visiting hours? HA-HA!"

The villain escapes in a cloud of exhaust. Batman is angry. "You won't be laughing for long, Joker," he says.

With no time to lose, Batman calls the Batplane via remote control. It arrives in minutes. Batman gets into the sleek and silent vehicle. *The Joker isn't the only one with an ace up his sleeve,* Batman thinks. He uses a high-tech tracking device to follow his foe. The Joker is headed all the way to Metropolis, the home of Batman's friend Superman!

Batman trails the Joker to the LexCorp building. The Joker and Lex Luthor have a private meeting. Perched on a ledge across the street, Batman spies on the villains. The Dark Knight learns that Luthor hired the Joker to destroy the Man of Steel.

"This little item is the key to Superman's undoing," Lex says, admiring the meteorite. "With him destroyed, Metropolis will be mine!"

"*Ours*," the Joker corrects. "Don't forget, I'm doing all the dirty work here so you can keep your hands clean."

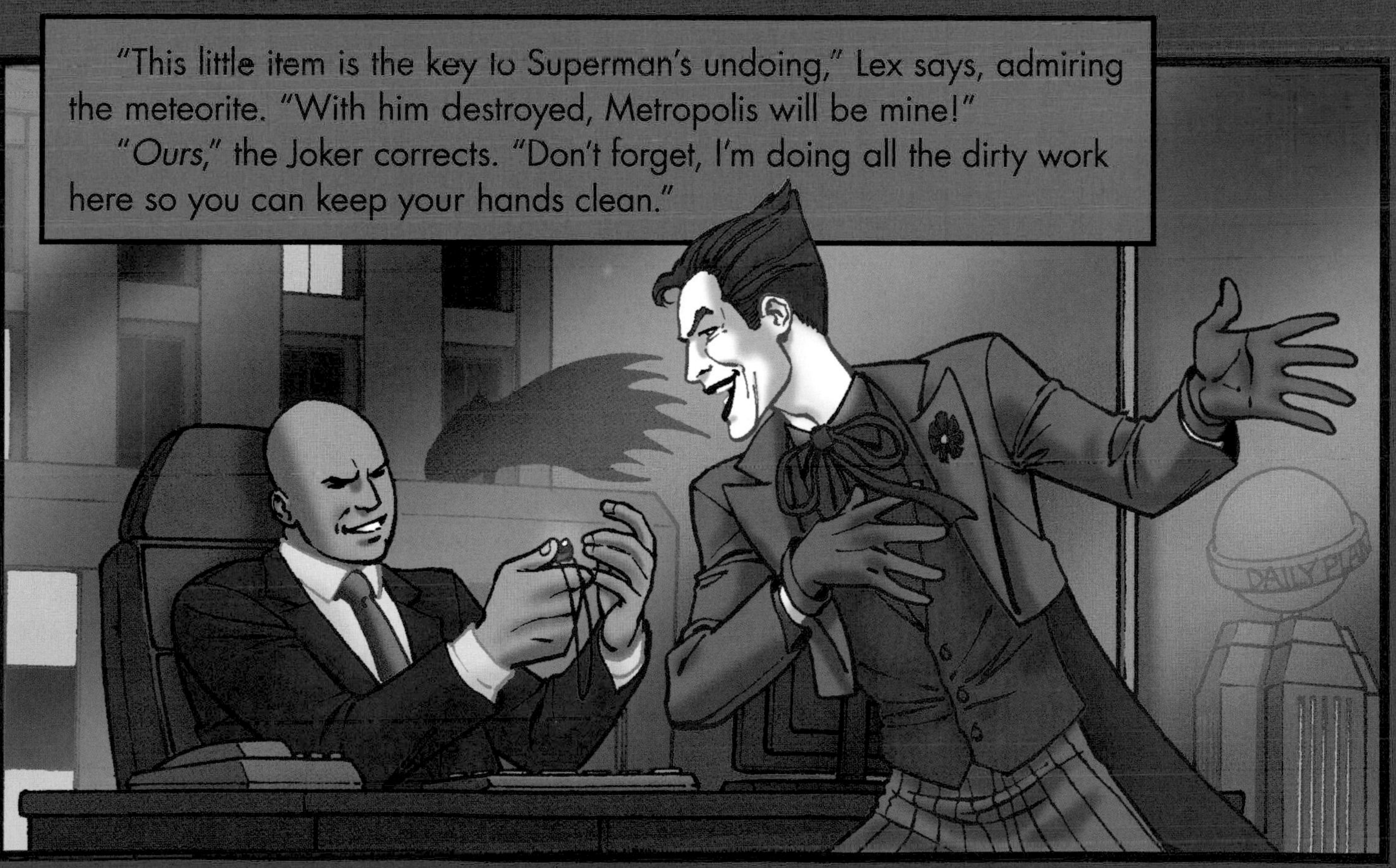

Batman immediately contacts Superman. They meet under the globe of the Daily Planet Building. Batman tells Superman what he knows.

"The Joker is very dangerous and unpredictable," Batman says to Superman. "Beware his next move."

"Likewise, Lex Luthor is crafty and cunning," Superman says. "I think it's time we teamed up to take them down."

"Agreed," Batman says.

Together, the world's finest heroes are ready for action!

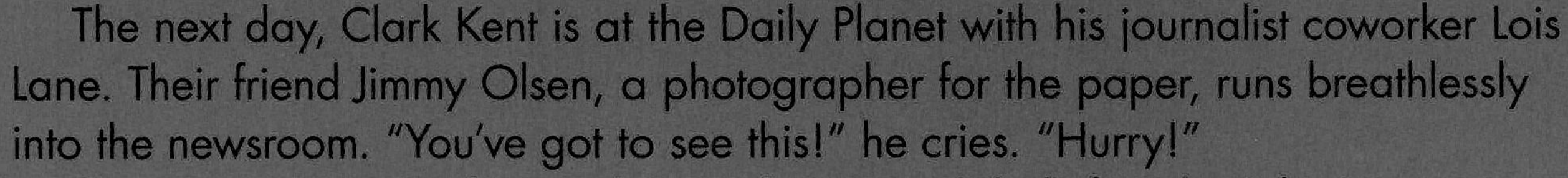
The next day, Clark Kent is at the Daily Planet with his journalist coworker Lois Lane. Their friend Jimmy Olsen, a photographer for the paper, runs breathlessly into the newsroom. "You've got to see this!" he cries. "Hurry!"
The reporters run to the window and stare in disbelief as the Joker's enormous blimp flies over their building. The Joker himself yells into a bullhorn. "I am no longer a one-town clown. I'm taking my creep show on a world tour. HA-HA-HA!"

"You've made your move, Joker,"
Clark says to himself. "Now it's my turn.
This looks like a job for Superman!"

Lex Luthor is having lunch at a fancy rooftop restaurant. When the Joker's blimp appears, the criminal clown disembarks and enters the dining area.
"Ladies and gentlemen," the Joker cries. "I am joining you for lunch!" He heads over to Luthor's table. "I'll order the bald billionaire, please . . . TO GO!"
"What is the meaning of this?" Luthor yells at the intruder.
"I like my meals *rich,*" the Joker says, and ties up Luthor with trick party streamers. Then he drags his partner toward the blimp.

In a blur of red and blue, the Man of Steel appears. "Just my luck." The Joker sneers. "Everywhere I go there's a big blockhead in long pajamas."
"Your luck has run out," Superman says sternly. "Now give up."

The Joker pretends to turn himself in and approaches Superman. Then the scoundrel slips the pendant around the hero's neck. "Here's a jewel for the flying fool!" The Joker giggles with glee.

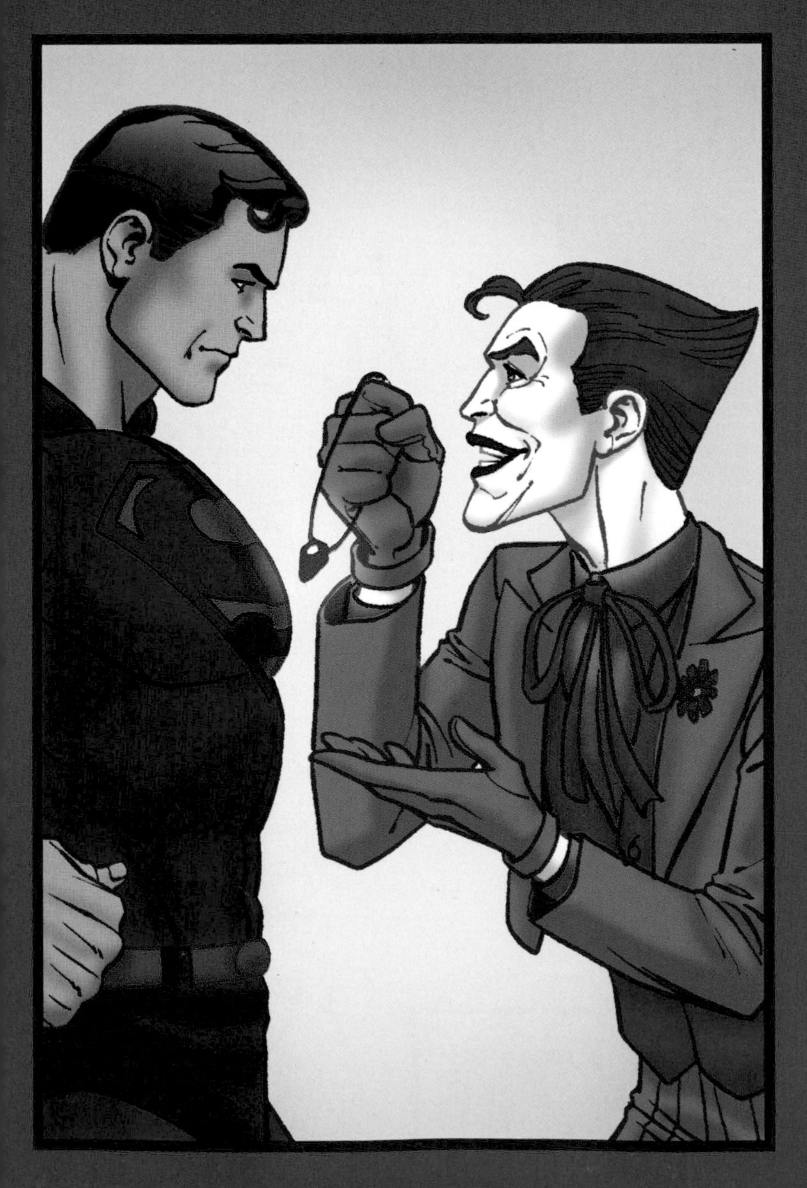

Instantly, Superman feels weak and falls to his knees. "The stone . . ." He gasps. "It's Kryptonite!" The hapless hero stumbles over the balcony ledge and plummets to the street below.

All of a sudden, a dark shape blocks out the sun. It's the Batplane! Rushing to Superman's side, Batman sees the glowing green rock. He knows that Kryptonite is a radioactive element deadly to the Man of Steel.

Batman pours acid on the stone, dissolving it.

"Thank you, friend," Superman says as he regains his strength. "Let's go burst the Joker's bubble."

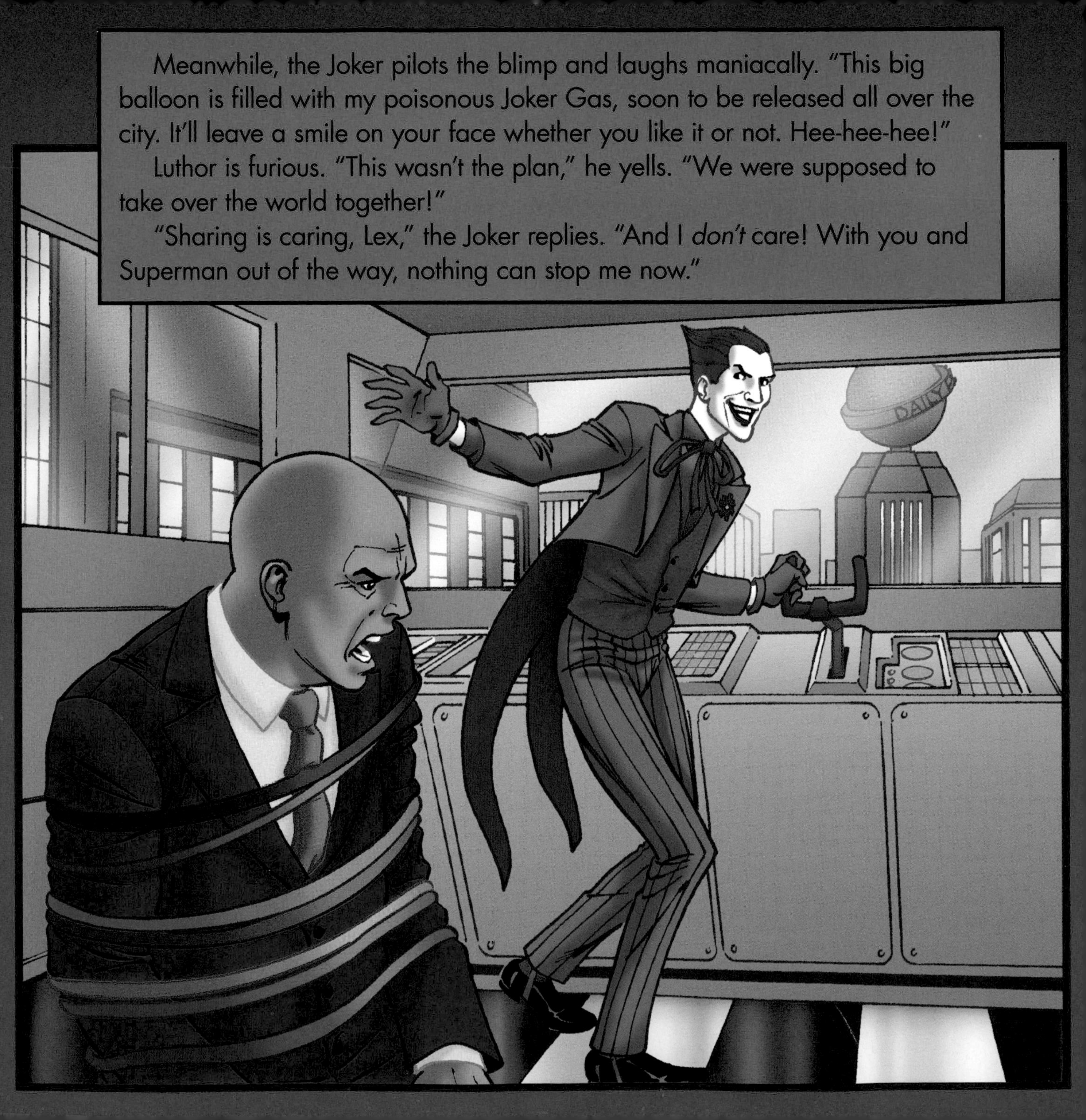
Meanwhile, the Joker pilots the blimp and laughs maniacally. "This big balloon is filled with my poisonous Joker Gas, soon to be released all over the city. It'll leave a smile on your face whether you like it or not. Hee-hee-hee!"
Luthor is furious. "This wasn't the plan," he yells. "We were supposed to take over the world together!"
"Sharing is caring, Lex," the Joker replies. "And I *don't* care! With you and Superman out of the way, nothing can stop me now."

Suddenly, Superman and Batman smash through
the wall of the blimp. "Guess again, Joker!" Superman
exclaims. "You're not the only one with a powerful partner."
"Another uninvited pest!" the Joker yells at Batman.
"Go haunt a house, you flying mouse!"
"Party's over," says Batman.

"The fun has just begun!" shouts the Joker. He reaches for the lever that will release the toxic gas. Superman blasts the control panel with his heat vision. ZAP!

Batman deftly delivers his Batarang and knocks the Joker off his feet. "Pop goes the weasel," Batman replies.

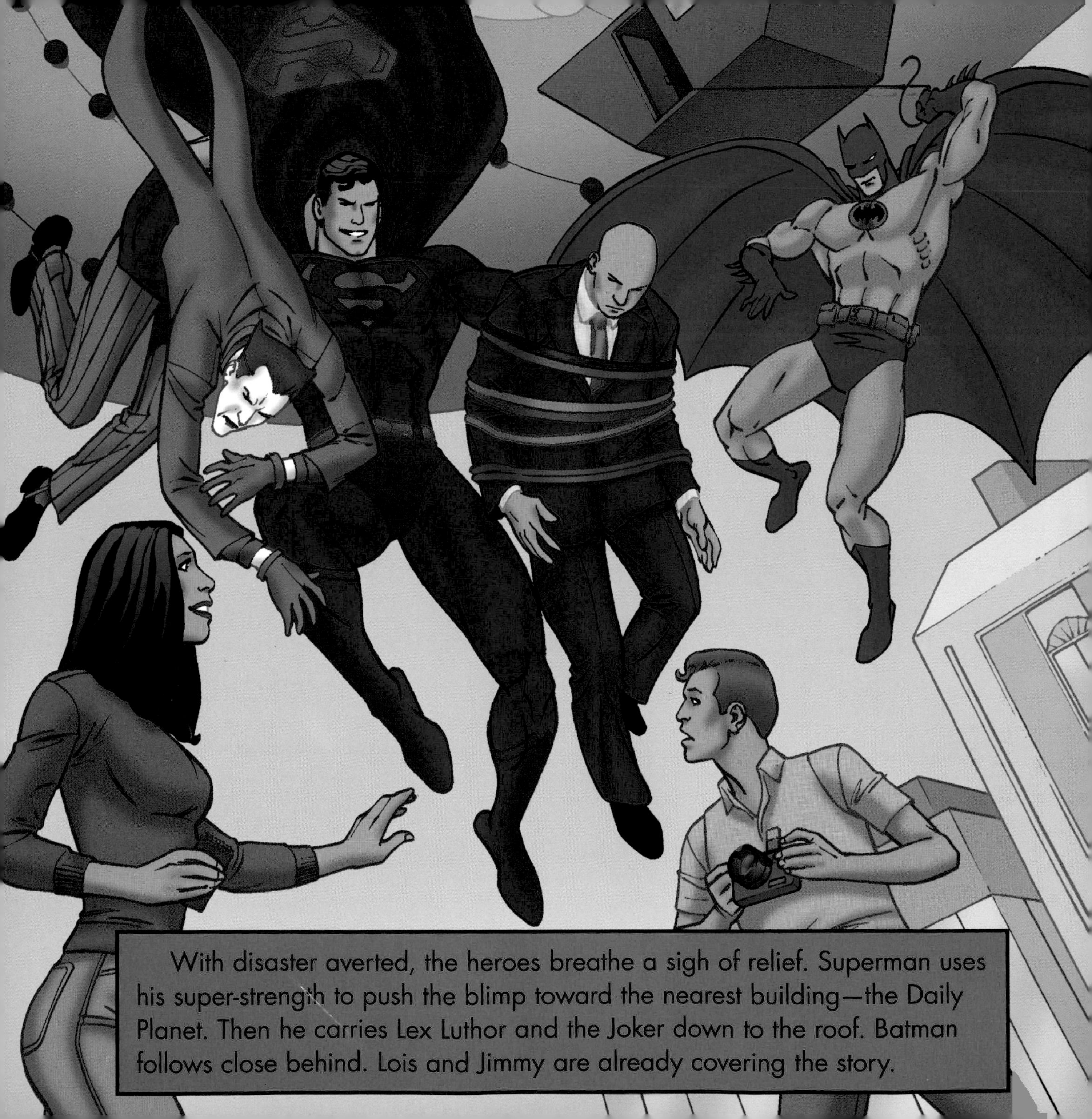
With disaster averted, the heroes breathe a sigh of relief. Superman uses his super-strength to push the blimp toward the nearest building—the Daily Planet. Then he carries Lex Luthor and the Joker down to the roof. Batman follows close behind. Lois and Jimmy are already covering the story.

Seeing the reporters, Luthor lays it on thick. "Thank you, Batman and Superman. You saved my life, and you saved the world!"

"Save it, Luthor," Batman growls. He produces evidence from his Utility Belt. "This is proof that you and the Joker teamed up to destroy Superman." Batman hands the pictures over to Lois Lane. The disgraced businessman boils with rage.

Moments later, the Metropolis police arrive and arrest the criminals.

"You're full of more hot air than that Joker blimp," Lois says to Luthor.

"That blimp will certainly light up the trophy room in my Fortress of Solitude," Superman adds.

"Take us away!" the Joker whines. "I can't stand any more of these corny jokes!"

Batman turns to leave. "I'd better get back to Gotham."

Superman stops him. "Gotham City is lucky to have a hero like you," he says, and shakes Batman's hand.

"Metropolis is lucky to have you, too," Batman replies.

"Gosh," says Jimmy. "We're lucky to have you both. What a terrific team-up!" He snaps a few photos of the heroes to commemorate the momentous event.

The next morning, Bruce Wayne is eating breakfast at his mansion in Gotham City. His butler, Alfred, walks in with the newspaper. "I see Superman helped Batman jail the Joker," he says.

"Indeed," replies Bruce. "And Batman helped Superman lock up Lex Luthor."

"Of course, Master Bruce," Alfred adds. "That's what *super* friends are for!"